David Jennings

An introduction to the knowledge of medals

David Jennings

An introduction to the knowledge of medals

ISBN/EAN: 9783742844644

Manufactured in Europe, USA, Canada, Australia, Japa

Cover: Foto ©Andreas Hilbeck / pixelio.de

Manufactured and distributed by brebook publishing software
(www.brebook.com)

David Jennings

An introduction to the knowledge of medals

A N

INTRODUCTION

TO THE

KNOWLEDGE

OF

MEDALS.

By the late Rev. *DAVID JENNINGS*, D. D.

LONDON:

Printed by *JOHN BASKERVILLE*;

For

T. FIELD, in Cheapſide; and J. PAYNE, in Pater-
noſter-Row. M DCC LXIV.

Advertiſement.

*A*S *the knowledge of Medals is confeſſed to be not only entertaining, but in ſeveral reſpeƈts of great uſe to the Chronologiſt, Hiſtorian, and Divine, as well as in particular to the Lovers and Profeſſors of the fine Arts; it is preſumed there is ſome ground to expeƈt the following little Treatiſe on that ſubjeƈt, will meet with a favourable reception from the Publick; to whom it is offered; not as containing any thing new, but as comprehending, in a ſmall compaſs, a compleat Introduƈtion to that Science; and as peculiarly calculated for thoſe, who deſiring a general acquaintance with the ſubjeƈt, have neither time nor opportunity for ſtudying larger Treatiſes, which enter into it more minutely. For the uſe of ſome young perſons ſo circumſtanced, it was originally drawn up; and it is now printed from the Author's Copy, correƈted by his own hand.*

THE

THE
CONTENTS.

Of

Of MEDALS.

§. 1. HISTORY of MEDALS.

BY Medals we underſtand, in general, ſuch Pieces in the form of Coin, as were either the Current Money of the Ancients; or ſtruck on particular occaſions, and deſigned to preſerve to poſterity the pourtrait of ſome Great Perſon, or the memory of ſome Illuſtrious Action.

Scaliger deriveth the word Medal from the Arabic *Methalia;* a ſort of Coin with a human head upon it.

But the opinion of *Voſſius* is generally received; *viz.* that it comes from *Metallum*, Metal; of which ſubſtance Medals are commonly made.

Some, indeed, apprehend that none of the Ancient Pieces we now ſtile Medals, were ever Current Coin, but all ſtruck on particular occaſions; like thoſe Modern Pieces which are called by that Name, to diſtinguiſh them from Common and Current Coin.

B   Others

Others are of a contrary opinion, as *Monfieur Patin*, and *Father Joubert*, who endeavour to prove, that they had all a regular and fixed Price in Payment.

But the much greater probability of the middle opinion hath obtained it the general vogue: According to which, Medals are diftinguifhed into two Sorts.

Of the firft fort fome are fuppofed to have been originally intended, either for *Miffilia*, which were fcattered among the People on Days of Triumph, Jubilees, and Solemn Proceffions, as is ufual among us at the Coronation: or for *Donativa*, of which Prefents were made to Princes, or their Ambaffadors, or to others in a way of honorary Reward, for fome worthy Action; as our *Royal Society* prefenteth every Year, a gold Medal to one of its Members, who hath diftinguifhed himfelf by fome valuable difcovery in Natural Philofophy. Others, which are of the moft exquifite workmanfhip, are fuppofed to be *Teftimonia probatæ monetæ;* that is, Effays of the wrokmanfhip of the Mint Mafters, which were prefented to their Princes and to perfons of the higheft Quality.

The fecond fort of which there is the greateft quantity, are taken to have been originally, the Current Coin of their refpective nations; but which

which through their fcarcity, are now laid up in
the cabinets of the curious.

Ancient Medals are often found in the ruins
of great buildings, in *Greece, Italy*, and other
Countries; where they are picked up, chiefly
after violent fhowers of rain, when being wafhed
from the dirt, they are more eafily difcovered.
They are often found in the Earth, by ploughing or diging; fometimes fingly, as having been
droped cafually; fometimes in Urns which are
filled with them. They are often alfo found in
ancient Roman Sepulchres; for Inftance, in the
Tumuli, or round mounts of Earth, about ten
or twelve feet high, which are feen by the fides
of publick Roads in fome parts of *England*; particularly, in *Leicefterfhire*. Thefe *Tumuli* are the
Sepulchres of Roman Officers, who were buried
there while their Legions were in that Country;
and are generally found cuped at the top, by their
having been dug for Urns and Medals. And for
the moft part wherever there have been Towns or
Incampments of the *Romans*, many of their
Coins are difcovered in the Earth by ploughing
or diging, particularly at *Silchefter* in *Hampfhire*
(The antient *Vindomis* of the *Romans*, of which
Profeffer *Ward* has given an account in the
Philofophical Tranfactions, No. 490) great
numbers

numbers have been found of all Metals, and
of all Sizes. One Gentleman in the neighbour-
hood is poffeffed of feveral hundreds collefted
from this Roman Settlement, and many of them
exceedingly well preferved. Nay, fo extenfive was
the commerce of the Roman Empire in its moft
flourifhing ftate, that there is hardly a country
in the world where its Coins have not been difcovered. Nor need we except even *America*, if
we may depend on what *Maurinus Siculus* relates
in his Hiftory of Spain, Cap. 19. *viz.* that a
Brafs Medal of the Emperor *Augustus* was found
in the Gold Mines of Brazil, and fent by the
Archbifhop of the Province to the Pope.

The Æra of the invention of Medals, or Coins
is not eafily fettled.

Villalpandus believes them to have been the
invention of *Tubal Cain*, becaufe otherways he
does not fee how it can be truly faid, that he
was *the Inftructor of every Artificer in Brafs and
Iron*, Gen. iv. 22. as if he, who found out the
art of melting thofe Metals, and making in-
ftruments of them, might not be ftiled the chief
Inftructor or Father of all the workmen of that
art; without having thought of every particular
ufe and purpofe, to which thofe Metals have
been fince applied.

The

The invention of Coin and Money was doubt-lefs of a later date: It is reafonable to fuppofe its firft ufe was in Trade and Commerce, and that its convenience for that purpofe gave rife to the invention.

The moft ancient way of traffic, was by truck-ing, or exchanging one commodity for another. Thus we read in *Homer, that Glaucus's* golden armour was valued at one hundred Cows; and *Diomedes*'s armour at ten.

From this ancient and ufual way of purchaf-ing, efpecially with cattle; *Bochart* conceives, that feveral *Greek* words relating to traffic, had their original: which words are no inconfider-able evidence that this was in fact, the ancient way of trading: in particular, ωνεισθαι emere απο των ονων Affes; πωλειν, vendere, απο των πωλων Nags; and αρνυσθαι, confequi, permutare, απο των αρνων Lambs.

But this being found inconvenient, both from the difficulty of adjufting the value of things, and many times, from the owner of one commo-dity, not wanting that which the other had to fpare; men devifed and agreed upon one particu-lar commodity to be the medium of their com-merce, and a common meafure for eftimating the value of all others: and this was *Metal*, efpeci-ally

ally *Copper*; which in thofe ancient times being in general ufe for making their defenfive armour, their houfhold veffels and other utenfils, every one was ready to exchange for it whatever he had to fpare.

That Copper was the firft Metal ufed for this purpofe among the *Romans*, not only appears from their hiftories, but from the word *Æs*, being afterwards ufed in their Language for Money in general. So likewife *Ærarium*, for a Treafury, and *Obæratus*, for one in debt, &c.

Yet the invention of Coins was not fo ancient, as this ufe of Metal for a medium of trade and commerce; but it was at firft paid μεγεθει και ςαθμω, as *Ariftotle* fpeaks, by bulk and weight. Hence the Latin words for paying, fpending, &c. come from *pendere*, to weigh; as *impendere*, *expendere*, *appendere*, &c. And fo the Hebrew word שקל Shekel, (which was the name of a certain Coin) comes from שקל Shakal, to weigh. But it being found troublefome to be continually weighing Metals, in exchange, in every bargain, pofterity contriv'd to fet a public ftamp on certain pieces, which fhould exprefs their weight, and confequently their value: fomewhat in the fame manner, perhaps, as the *Swedes* ftamp their Copper-money at this day. This method is faid by

fome

fome to have been introduced among the *Romans*
by *Numa Pompilius;* from whence, they tell us,
money thus ftamp'd was call'd *Nummus;* though
others derive that name from the Greek word
νομ☉, *Lex;* denoting its being eftablifhed by
law. This may perhaps fuggeft to us the mean-
ing of an expreffion in Gen. xxiii. 16. where
the four hundred Shekels of filver, which *Abraham*
paid to *Ephron* for the field and cave of *Machpe-
lah*, are faid to be *current money with the merchant:*
that is, mark'd with the public ftamp, which
made it current at a known value. And though
Abraham is indeed faid to *weigh* this filver to
Ephron; yet, why may we not fuppofe, that the
Hebrew word שקל is us'd in the fame manner as
the Latin verb *appendo*, viz. for paying money,
even after the more ancient cuftom of weighing
it was laid afide. And if fo, the argument will
fail, by which fome have endeavour'd to prove,
that all Jewifh Coins pretending to higher antiquity than the Babylonifh captivity, muft needs
be fpurious: Becaufe, as it is faid, the *Jews* had
no Coins before the captivity, but continued the
ancient cuftom of weighing the Metals they gave
in exchange for commodities. For proof of which
is alledged, Jer. xxxii. 9. where *Jeremiah* is faid
to have " weighed to *Hanameel* the price of the
" field

" field which he bought of him." But as in that text, Shakal, which we render to *weigh*, is literally tranflated by the Latin word *appendo;* why may we not fuppofe it is ufed in the fame latitude? namely, for *paying* of money, as well as *weighing*.

Thus far we have endeavoured to trace out the origin of money; taking reafonble probability for our guide, where certain evidence is not to be had. But we have hardly fo good a guide to follow in difcovering the firft inventor of Coins.

The Greeks, refer the invention to *Hermodice,* wife of King *Midas.*

The Latins, to *Numa,* as was faid before.

Others, to *Janus* or *Saturn.*

But the Jews who muft needs furpafs all other nations both in antiquity, and in the honour of inventions, refer it to *Abraham,* if not to higher antiquity. For they tell·us in *Berefchith Rabba,* and in other Books, that *Abraham* coined money in his day; and for proof of it they produce fome Coins with the pourtraits of an old man and old woman· on one fide, for *Abraham* and *Sarah;* and a young man and young woman on the other fide, for *Ifaac* and *Rebeccah.*

How the firft [Money was ftamped, and with what marks and charaƈters, is not known. However

er among the Romans *Pliny* relates, L. 18.
ap. 3. that *Servius Tullus*, the fixth King of
ome, was the firft that ftamped Images on their
oin; viz. the figure of an Ox, a Sheep, or a
wine: from whence, they fay, Money was called
ecunia, from the old word *Pecu*, Cattle.

Some imagine the Image on the Coin was in-
nded to denote its value, as being the ordinary
rice of the creature whofe image it bore. How-
er that be, it is certain, the like ftamps had
een ufed more anciently, by the Greeks; from
hom it is probable King *Tullus* borrow'd them.

Some afcribe a higher antiquity to thefe fort of
oins, than[†] either *Greeks* or *Romans*; for they
nd them in the hiftory of *Jacob*, Gen. xxxiii. 19.
here it is faid, that *Jacob bought a parcel of a*
ld of the children of Hamor for one hundred קְשִׂיטָה
efitah, which we tranflate, *Pieces of money*: but
l the ancient verfions, viz. the *Septuagint, Vul-*
te, Syriac, Arabic, and the *Targum of Onkelos,*
nder it lambs or fheep. Now that thefe *Kefitah*
ere not real lambs, (though that is the opinion
f *Onkelos, Aben–Ezra,* and *Pagnin)* is argu'd by
ochart, *Hieroz*. *Part* 1ft. *L.* 2d. *C.* 43. on the
llowing reafons,

1ft. Becaufe the way of trucking, or bartering
ods for goods, had been laid afide, and the ufe

† the times of the

of money in bargains introduced before *Jacob*'s time, as appears from Gen. xvii. 12 13. Cap. xxiii. 16. and in his days we have more in-stances than one of the ufe of money as Gen. xxxvii. 28. Cap. xlii. 27. Cap. xliii. 12. There-fore it is not probable, that he bought the field with Lambs, contrary to the prevailing cuftom, but with money.

2dly. Though Lambs and Sheep are fpoken of more than one hundred times in other Texts of Scripture, as in the laws about facrifices, and in the Prophets; yet they are never once called by this Word *Kefitah*.

3dly. There is only one place more where the word *Kefitah* is ufed, (except in the recital of *Jacob*'s purchafe of the field, Jofhua xxiv. 32.) and that is, Job. xlii. 2. where we read, that when *Job*'s friends came to comfort him, after his loffes and afflictions, *every man gave him a Kefitah*, and *every one an Ear-ring of Gold.* Now it is hardly probable, that towards repairing his lofs of feven Thoufand Sheep; Chap. i. 3. his friends fhould contribute no more than a fingle Lamb a piece; or that they would have joined fo trifling a prefent, as a Lamb, with an Ear-ring of Gold.

4thly. If we fuppofe *Kefitah* to fignify Lambs,
the

the feminine termination makes it neceſſary for us to underſtand it only of female Lambs. Now it is not very probable, that either *Jacob* ſhould pay for his field, or that *Job* ſhould be preſented by his friends, with ſuch only.

But 5th. The moſt concluſive argument is taken from Acts vii. 16. where *Stephen,* in relating this purchaſe of the field which *Jacob* made, of the ſons of *Emmor,* ſaith, it was bought not with Lambs or Sheep, but τιμης αργυριον with a ſum of money. Therefore, theſe *Keſitah* were undoubtedly pieces of Money; the word being probably deriv'd from קשט *Veritas,* denoting *Proba Monæta,* as the *Romans* expreſſed it, or true Standard Money in reſpect to weight and Metal. And as the Silver Penny, the only Coin formerly uſed in *England,* was call'd a *Sterling,* being a certain ſtandard in reſpect of weight and fineneſs: (the word *Sterling,* according to *Somner,* being derived from the Saxon *Steore,* a Rule or Standard.) So in *Jacob*'s time, there very likely might be only one ſort of Coin in that country, ſtiled *Keſitah,* for the ſame reaſon the *Engliſh* Penny was called a *Sterling.* But how then came the ancient tranſlators to render *Keſitah,* Lambs? *Grotius,* with ſeveral others, ſuppoſeth that the *Keſitah* being ſtamped with the figure of a Lamb, it was therefore called

C 2   by

by that name: As one ancient Athenian Coin was calld βυς, an Ox; another γλαυκες, that is, γλαυκωδης, *Noctuæ Speciem gerens*, from γλαυξ, an Owl; and as our broad pieces of Gold were called *Jacobus's*, and *Carolus's*, from the figure ſtamp'd upon them. But that the ancient Hebrew or Phænician *Keſitah* was ſtamp'd with the figure of a Lamb, is *Gratis Dictum:* at leaſt there is no other reaſon to ſuppoſe it, but the ancient verſions redering *Keſitah*, a Lamb.

However, *Bochart* mentions another, and perhaps more probable reaſon for this rendering of the word *Keſitah* in the ancient verſions: Namely, that it was owing to a corruption of the Seventy, which originally read εκατον μνων, *centum minis*, or Pounds. But ſome Tranſcriber, through careleſſneſs or miſtake, happening to prefix an α to μνων, turn'd it into αμνων, Lambs. And I think it probable that other Tranſlators not rightly underſtanding the word *Keſitah*, it being next to an απαξ λεγομενον, for that reaſon the more eaſily followed this corruption of the Septuagint. There is a ſimilar inſtance in Gen. xxxi. 7. taken notice of by St. *Auſtin* and *Jerom*, though they knew not how to account for a rendering, which to them appeared very ſtrange.

Whether any of the Hebrew Coins now extant are

are genuine, is doubted by some skilful Medalists.
It is certain, that in the New Testament there is
no mention of any Coins in use among the Jews,
besides Grecian and Roman; which may lead
one to suspect, that the many Shekels now shewn
with Hebrew characters, and pretended to have
been the Money of that nation, are counterfeit,
and of a later origin than the age of the New
Testament history. That which is least suspect-
ed, is what is commonly called the Shekel
of the Sanctuary, about the bigness of an *English*
Half Crown;, having on one side, as some con-
ceive, the pot of Manna, or as others suppose, the
Censer, or *Thuribulum;* and on the other side, a
sprig of the *Opobalsamum;* or else the Rod of
Aaron that budded; with a legend on one side,
signifying *the Shekal of Israel;* and on the other,
Jerusalem the Holy; and both in ancient Samaritan Characters. If it may be depended upon
that this Coin is genuine, (as several learned men
are persuaded it is) it will go a great way towards
determining the controversy in favour of the antiquity of the Samaritan, in preference to the pre-
sent square Hebrew or Chaldee character: as we
have elsewhere observed, *viz.* in the *Appendix to
the Lectures on Jewish Antiquities, concerning the
Language of the Jews.*

Among

Among the Medals or Coins of other nations,
thofe of the Greeks and Romans have in a manner engrofs'd the attention of the Connoiffeurs.
However we muft by no means overlook the *Perfian Darics*, which are commonly reckon'd indeed
among the Greek Medals, and are fo called from
Darius, whofe head they bear, with, fometimes;
a *Sagittarius*, or Bow-man on the reverfe, and
fometimes, a rowing Galley : efpecially fince (as
Raphelius thinks) they are mentioned in Scripture, 1 Chron. xxix. 7. and Ezra viii. 27. where
he underftands by אדרכנים the *Perfian Darics*, or,
as the Grecians call them, *δαρικ8ς*, though our
Tranflators have confounded them with the
דרכמוים or Attick Drams, mentioned alfo, Ezra
ii. 69. Nehem. vii. 70, 72. Vide *Rephelii Anno-
tationes, Tom. 1ft. P. 20.*

Of the ancient Greek Coins, both of their
Kings and Republicks, there are great numbers
ftill extant of all the ufual Metals ; many of them
with little elegancy ; yet others with a more exquifite Relievo, than the Romans, who coppied
the Greeks, could ever equal. The Gold Coins
of the Greeks are of the fmaller fize ; but their
Copper ones of all fizes, are found in almoft all
countries ; their extenfive conquefts, efpecially under *Alexander the Great*, having been the means of
                                    difperfing

difperfing them wherever their armies came.
Some of them bear the Image of their Emperors,
as the *Philippei*, the *Alexandrei*, &c. or the pourtraits of their victorious Generals, and others,
the Signatures and Emblems of the places they
conquered. There are fome Greek Coins with
Latin infcriptions; and others, though very few,
with Greek on the one fide, and Latin on the
other.

As upon the decline of the *Greecian*, and the
rife of the *Roman* Empire, all other ufeful and
polite arts migrated from *Greece* to *Rome*, fo did
this of Coining. The firft money of the *Romans*
is faid to have been nothing but Plates of Copper ftamped with fome mark, which fignified
their weight and value. But of that fort there
are none now remaining. Some of thefe Plates
were of a pound weight, which they called *As;*
fome of two pound, which they called *Dupon-
dium;* others were parts of the *As* or pound,
which they divided into twelve *Unciæ* or ounces;
as the *Sextans*, the fixth Part of the *As*, or two
ounces; the *Quadrans*, the fourth Part, or three
ounces; *Triens*, four ounces; *Sæmis* or *Selibra*,
fix ounces, or half an *As*, &c. This was the
ftate of their money till the firft Carthaginian
War, when the Treafury being exhaufted, and
the

the Commonwealth much in debt, they raifed it to fix times its former value; fo that now the *As* weighed but two ounces. About this time it is fuppofed the Effigies of the *Pecus* on their Coins began to be laid afide; and inftead of it, they ftamped a Two Faced Janus on one fide, and a Beak or Stern of a fhip, on the other. When afterwards they were brought into great diftrefs by *Hannibal,* the *As* was again leffened to one ounce; and after a while it was reduced by the *Papyrian Law* to half an ounce; of which fort a great number of *Roman* As's are to be feen at this day. The *As* thus reduced was alfo divided into fmaller Coins for the eafe of the people; as into the *Dodrans,* or three quarters: The Quadrans, or one quarter. On the Quadrans one fometimes fees the Stern of a *Rates* or Ferry-Boat: this was called *Quadrans Ratitus;* being the Fare, which was ordinarily paid for paffage by water from the City to *Mount Aventine,* from which it was anciently feparated by a lake.

Silver Money is faid to have been firft coined by the Romans, Anno. U. C. four hundred and eighty four, five years before the firft Carthaginian War. The largeft piece, weighing about the feventh part of an ounce, was the *Denarius,* equal in value to ten As's; and therefore marked with

with an X, the numerical letter for ten. The *Denarius*, was again fubdivied into the *Quinarius*, and *Seftertius;* the former being half the *Denarius*, the latter one quarter.

'Afterwards, in the fecond Carthagenian War, the *Denarius* was raifed to the value of fixteen *As's*, and the leffer divifions of it in proportion; as appeareth by the marks on fome of thofe pieces now extant.

As for Gold, it was fcarce with the Romans; and no Coins were ftruck of that Metal till thirteen years, faith *Pliny;* others fay, till fixty-two years after the Coining of Silver. Thefe were diftinguifhed into the *Aurius* or *Denarius. Aurius*, equal in weight to two Silver Denarii, and in value to twenty four; and into the *Se-miffes* and *Tremiffes;* though it is faid, that none of thefe two latter Coins were ftruck 'till the time of *Alexander Severus*.

Neither the Greeks nor Romans permitted any perfon to coin money in private, and without the authority of the ftate. They had publick Mints appointed in divers places, which the Greeks called *Argyrocopia;* the Romans, *Argentaria.* The Moneyers, or Coiners, were called *Monetarii.* There was fuch a Mint at *Lyons* in *France*, where the Romans, during their wars with the Gauls, coin-

D   ed

ed money for the payment of ther army: and there feveral Earthen Moulds have been dug up, with the heads of Roman Emperors, and other Illuftrious Perfons, as *Alexander Severus, Geta, Julia Pia,* &c. which may fuggeft to us a hint concerning their manner of coining, that it probably was by cafting the Metal in thofe moulds ; and afterwards fmoothing and finifhing them with a Dye, or Stamp, while they were hot: And this accounts for fo many of the Roman Copper Coins being cracked at the edges.

Both Greeks and Romans had ordinarily a Mint in the capital of every province; and we often find the place of the coinage expreffed in the infcription; as *Lugduni* on a Coin of *M. Antoninus.* Another has the letters P. TR. for *Percuffa. Treveris.* One of *Helena,* the mother of *Conftantine,* has C. O. N. OB. for *Conftantinopoli obfignata:* And the like of feveral other cities.

The workmen, or coiners, were under the direction of certain Controulers, or Mint-Mafters; who were called the Triumviri, becaufe there were ordinarily three of them, tho' fometimes their number was increafed to four or five. Thefe were men of figure and authority, infomuch that they frequently ftamped their own names, and fometimes their heads, upon the Coins they
ftruck,

I.

ſtruck, with the A. A. A. F. F. for *Auro Argento, Ære, Flando feriundo:* ſignifying it to be their office to overſee the coining of theſe ſeveral Metals into money. But as the Triumviri derived their power from the ſenate and people, the permiſſion or authority of the ſenate is commonly expreſſed on the Medal by the letters S. C. which ſtand for *Senatus Confulto.* On a Medal of *Tiberius* we find the letters N. C. A. P. R. which probably ſtand for *Nobis conceſſum a populo Romano;* tho' ſome read it *non conceſſum,* &c. The S. C. on Medals is by ſome apprehended to denote that thoſe ſo marked were current coin, by which they were diſtinguiſhed from the *Miſſilia, Donativa,* &c.

SECTION the SECOND:

OF THE

Matter, Size, *and* Shape

Of MEDALS.

Firſt. THE matter or ſubſtance of ancient Medals is commonly one of the three Metals ſignified by the three A's, which, on ſeveral Coins, are placed after the name of the Mint-maſter; namely, Gold, Silver, and Copper or Braſs, commonly, I ſay; for ſome Medals are ſaid to have been found of Iron. Yet I cannot ſuppoſe, that if there were ſuch formerly, many of them can be now remaining; becauſe that Metal is ſo ſubject to decay with ruſt. There are many Silver Coins to be met with, debaſed below the proper ſtandard. In the declenſion of the Roman Empire, when there was a ſcarcity of the Richer Medals, this was ſometimes done by authority, in order to raiſe money to pay the army; which

which at times occafioned feditions among them. For the like purpofe, when our King *James* II. was diftreffed for Money, during the war in *Ireland*, he coined Copper Shillings, and Half Crowns. However, amongft the Romans, this was fometimes done clandeftinely, by the knavery of the Mint-Mafters, or Coiners; notwithftanding it was made a capital crime. Thus *Pliny* writes, that when *M. Antoninus* was Triumvir, he mixed Iron with the Denarii, which fhould have been all Silver. But the moft common mixture in the Bafe Coin is that of Copper or Brafs. We fometimes meet with Old Coins little better than Lead: and fome tell us, that *Numa* ftamped Money of Leather: But no fuch Coins are to be found at this day.

As for the Æs, (the firft and moft common Metal ufed in Coinage,) it is diftinguifhed into three forts, viz. the Red Copper, the Yellow or Brafs, and the Pot-metal, which was Copper mixed with Tin or Lead. Before *Alex. Severus*, moft Coins were of the two former forts; but after him, almoft all are of the laft.

The fecond fort, or yellow, is alfo diftinguifhed into the common Brafs on Kettle-metal, and the Corinthian Brafs; which is faid by *Pliny* to be an accidental mixture of Metal, at the fack

and

and burning of *Corinth* by *Mummius* the Roman;
when the Gold, Silver, and Brafs Statues, and
all things made of Metal, being melted and
running together into low places, compofed that
mixed Metal, which is of a much finer colour
than common Brafs, and for its beauty, hath
been efteemed little inferior to Gold. But fome
Refiners, who have ftriclly examined this Metal
can find no Gold in it; and therefore juflly look
upon this account to be fabulous. Whether it
was a mixed, or fimple Metal, is not now known.
If it was *Mixed*, we have not been able to find
fo beautiful a compofition; if *Simple*, probably
the mines that produced it, have been long fince
exhaufted.

There are alfo fome Medals compofed of two
different Metals, not by melting them together,
but either by plating over Brafs or Iron with
Silver, (a fort of falfe money, that had it's rife
in the Triumvirate of *Auguftus;*) or by laying a
rim of a different Metal round the edge of a
Medal. Medals of this fort, which are all of the
larger fize, are called by the Antiquaries, *Contor-
niati*, from which is derived the French word
Contour; fignifying the out-line that determines
and defines a figure. It cannot be fuppofed thefe
were ever intended for common Coin, becaufe
the

the workmanſhip of them would come to more than they would be worth in currency: Nor are they ſuppoſed to be very ancient. *Father Hardouin* allows them no higher Antiquity than the thirteenth Century; others date them from the fifth; and others make them as ancient as the time of *Nero*.

Secondly. The ſize of the ancient Medals is from three inches to a quarter of an inch. Thoſe of the larger ſize, or Volume, as the Medaliſts expreſs it, ſome of which weigh two ounces and a half, are called *Medallions*: Of which ſort ſcarcely any are to be met with in Gold, few in Silver, but many in Copper. Theſe are not ſuppoſed to have ever been current Coin, but to be ſtruck on ſuch particular occaſions, and for ſuch purpoſes, as our Modern Medals are. As to the Size of other Medals, there is almoſt an endleſs variety betwixt the greateſt and the leaſt. However they are ranked into three claſſes, viz. *Large*, *Middle*, and *Small*; though it is ſometimes diffi-cult to aſſign a particular Medal to its proper claſs. The claſs of a Medal is not ſo much de-termined by its Breadth and Thickneſs, as by the Head that is ſtamped upon it. So that in caſe one of the Firſt Size for Breadth and Subſtance, bears a Head no bigger than one of the Middle

Size,

Size, or Bronze, as they call it; it is to be ranked in the Middle Clafs.

Thirdly. The Shape of Medals is round, or rather roundifh; for the Ancients had not the way of making their Money fo perfectly round as ours. The two fides, or Tables of the Medal, are diftinguifhed into the *Face* and the *Reverfe;* the Face bearing the chief Figure, as the Pourtrait of fome Emperor, or other Illuftrious Perfon: The Reverfe, fome Emblem, Infcription, or other Device, of which we fhall treat in another Section.

SECTION

SECTION the THIRD.

OF

The ORDERS into which

MEDALS are to be diftinguifhed.

MEDALS may be diftinguifhed,

1ft. By the Metal of which they are made.
2dly. By their different Sizes.
3dly. By the Nation to which they belonged.
4thly. By the Ages in which they were ftruck.

The two former diftinctions have been already confidered.

3dly. As to the Third we propofe to treat only of the Greek and Roman Medals, and chiefly of the latter. Here again it will be convenient to diftinguifh Medals into two Claffes, viz. Thofe of the State, and thofe of particular Cities and Colonies: For befides the Money coined by the State, it appears, that divers Cities and Colonies,

E   had

had the privilege of coining; where it is probable the chief magiſtrate was the Mint-Maſter. Father *Hardouin* has publiſhed a large Catalogue of Grecian and Roman Medals of this ſort, in a Quarto Volume, intitled, *Nummi Antiqui populorum et Urbium Illuſtrati:* which is a valuable work; but it would have been much more entertaining and uſeful, if he had explained the Devices and Inſcriptions of all the Medals in his Catalogue, as he has done of ſome of them. However this, Mr. *Vaillant* has done in two Volumes of the Latin Colonies, in which he has alſo given us Cuts of the Medals themſelves.

Among the Roman Colonies, ſome had *Jus Civitatis*; that is, the right of Roman Citizens; which conſiſted in a capacity of ſtanding for all offices of ſtate, and of enjoying all other privileges of the Citizens of *Rome.* Such a Colony was called *Municipium.* Of this kind was *Philippi:* Therefore the *Philippians* call themſelves *Romans*, Acts xvi. 21. While other Colonies, according to *Ulpian,* had little more than the name; enjoining only what they call, *Jus Italicum,* or *Jus Latii;* that is, they were free from the tributes and taxes payed by the Provinces, and were capable of ſerving in the Roman Legions. The former were more properly called Colonies, the
latter

latter only free Cities. Among the former, feveral learned men have fuppofed, was *Tarfus* in *Ci-
licia,* where *Paul* was bom; and that therefore
he had the privilege of a Roman Free-man by
birth, Acts xxii. 28. This opinion is efpoufed
by *Baronius, Hammond, Tillemont,* and *Witfius;* as
it was by Baron *Spanheim,* when he publifhed the
Quarto Edition of his Book, *De Præflantia et Ufu
Numifmatum,* An. 1671. But it appears he had
altered his opinion, when he publifhed his *Orbis
Romanus,* 1703. The chief evidence on which
he relied, when he wrote his former Book, was a
Medal of the Emperor *Gordianus* in the French
Kings collection, faid by *Monfieur Patin* to have
this infcription, ΚΟΛ ΕΛΕΤΘ ΤΑΡC. But
Spanheim was informed afterwards, that ΚΟΛ is
not in the legend of that Medal; nor indeed if it
were, would it prove, that *Tarfus* was a Colony
when *Paul* was bom, though it might have been
made fo by the time *Gordian* reigned. *Pliny* indeed calls *Tarfus* a *free City,* Lib. 5. Cap. 27.
But that is no evidence of its being a Colony
with *Jus Civitatis;* but rather the contrary, fince
if it had been fuch a Colony, or Municipium, it
is probable he would have called it fo. Therefore fome other learned men, particularly, *Grotius, Le Clerc,* and Dᵣ *Lardner,* think it neceffary

to account for St. *Paul's* being free born in some
other manner than merely by his being a native
of *Tarsus;* either by his Father, or some other
of his Ancestors, having purchased that freedom;
or by their being rewarded with it for some signal
service to the state. See *D*ˡ *Lardner's Cred. of
the Gos. Hist. Vol.* 1ʃ*t. P.* 483 *to* 493. Yet, on the
other hand, several testimonies are alledged from
antient writers in favour of *Tarsus* being a Colony
with *Jus Civitatis;* as that of *Dion Cassius,* L. 47.
who says, " The inhabitants of *Tarsus* were so
" friendly to *Julius Cæsar* (and on his account to
" *Augustus)* that from him they called themselves
" *Juliopolis.*" *Dio Chrysostom* also saith in his 34th
Oration, " Therefore whatever any one could
" confer on his Friends and Confederates, who
" had manifested so great an attachment to him,
" *Augustus* hath conferred on you, namely, Ter-
" ritory Laws, Honour, the property (or domi-
" nion) of the River, and of the neighbouring
" Sea" And the ancient *Greek Scholiast,* upon
2 Tim. iv. 13. tells us, that the citie of *Tarsus*
received this freedom, because they met the Roman Ambassadors with peace and crowns; and
that then the Father of *Paul* going with them received the *Pænula,* which he saith, was the φελονης
Paul desired to have with him, as the badge of
his

his freedom; inafmuch as he had fometimes occafion to infift on his Privilege as a Roman Ci-
tizen.

The Medals belonging to Cities were fo numerous, that above two hundred may ftill be
collected, of the *Greek Cities* only. Nay, not only
had feveral Cities, both among the Greeks and
Romans, the privilege of coining money, but
Generals of Armies frequently did it for the
fpeedy payment of their troops. And it fhould
feem by a paffage of *Suetonius,* in his life of *Tiberius,* Cap. 49. That this liberty was fometimes
granted to private perfons; for he there fpeaks
of *Veteres Immunitates, et Jus Metallorum et
Vectigalium pluribus Civitatibus et privatis adempta.*
But may it not admit of a Query, whether the
Coins thus privately ftruck were intended as
money, for publick ufe; or only for fuch pur-
pofes, for which Medals among us are often
ftruck by private hands. And if the latter be the
cafe, we can the better account for the vaft variety of Devices and Mottos we find upon Medals
of the fame reign, and why fo many of them ap-
pear without any of thofe marks of publick
authority, which others have.

4*thly,* Medals are ranked in different claffes
according to the ages when they were ftruck, as
the

the time of the *Kings*, the *Confuls*, and the *Em-perours*.

Of the firft fort, viz. Medals of the Kings, we have a great many Greek ones; of which Monf. *Vaillant* has given us a Catalogue; with Cuts of about one hundred and twenty of them. Thofe of the Kings of *Macedonia* yield in nothing to the moft exquifite workmanfhip of the Romans. There are alfo Coins ftill extant, of the Kings of *Pontus*, *Cappadocia*, *Bithynia*, *Thrafia*, and many others. But we have no Roman Medals ftruck in the time of their Kings; though many with their Pourtraits upon them. Thefe were ftruck by their Defcendants in after ages, in honour of their Royal Anceftors, and in order to eternize the Nobility of their own families. Thus we have a Medal of *Ancus Marcius*, the fourth King of *Rome*, which was ftruck by *L. Marcius Philippus*, one of his Defcendants, who was Conful, U. C. 662, about five hundred years after the death of *Ancus*..

2*d.* Confular Medals, or thofe that were ftruck during the Government of the Confuls, from the expulfion of *Tarquin* the laft King, to the beginning of the Empire under *Julius Cæfar*, containing the fpace of four hundred and ninety-four years.

The number of Roman Medals ftill extant, fup-

fuppofed to have been ftruck in this inter-
val, amount to about one thoufand five hundred;
moft of them Silver, and of the fmaller fize; for
of this clafs, we do not find above fifty or fixty
in Gold, and hardly more than two hundred and
fifty in Copper; of which Metal there are indeed
fome of all three fizes.

As the Confular Medals have tranfmitted to us
the names of feveral Roman Families, they are
called *Family Medals.* Some have fuppofed thefe
names to be thofe of the Confuls, under whofe
refpective Government the Medals are coined;
But that does not feem to have been the cafe:
For we have no Medals that bear the name of the
firft Confuls for more than two hundred years.
And as for thofe which bear the name of fuch
perfons, as we learn from the *Fafti* were Confuls;
yet they do not feem to have been ftruck in the
time of their Confulfhip; for we have often the
letters *Q.* or *P.* after the name, fignifying *Quæftor,*
or *Prætor;* (which was an office incompatible
with the Confulfhip,) and fometimes *Triumvir:*
Thefe names therefore were more probably, either
the names of the *Triumviri,* who coined the
Pieces; or of their Illuftrious Anceftors, many
of whom had been Conful; whofe names and
memory they endeavoured by this means to perpetuate.   The

The Confular Medals are reckoned to be the moft ancient of the Roman Coins now extant; and yet thofe of Copper and Silver are not fuppofed to be more ancient than the 484th year of *Rome;* nor thofe of Gold than the year 546. Whatever Medals, therefore, are produced of an older date, are looked upon as fpurious.

3*dly.* Imperial Medals, down from *Julius Cæfar,* (who put an end, though not to the name, yet the power of the Confuls) to the end of the Roman greatnefs, are diftinguifhed into thofe of the *Higher* and *Lower* Empire: the *Higher Empire* being reckoned from *Julius Cæfar* to the thirty Tyrants inclufively, or at fartheft to the end of the third Century of the Chriftian Æra. The *Lower Empire* from thence to the end of the ninth Century; none later being accounted ancient. Nor are the claffes of modern Medals reckoned to begin till the fifteeneth Century. As for thofe that were ftruck in the intermediate ages betwixt the 9th and the 15th, they are fo extremely rude and barbarous, that they deferve no regard. It was not till the fifteeneth Century that the curiofity of Medals, either as to the making or ftudy of them, begain to revive; being firft fet on foot by certain Painters, *Pifani, Boldue,* and others. Towards the middle of that age fome Medals were

ftruck

ſtruck with confiderable elegance, both of Defign
and Relief, as one of *Ferdinand*, King of *Arragon*,
An. 1449, and another of *John*, Emperor of *Con-
ſtantinople*, ten years before. But to return to the
Ancient Medals.

The gradual declenfion of the Roman taſte
and politenefs, is in nothing more fenfible than
in its Coins; which in the time of the lower Empire, in comparifon of what they had been formerly, grow to be very mean. The Bulk and
Size is thin and fmall; the Relievo, flat and low,
and without any thing of that elegance we fo
juſtly admire in the device and infcriptions of
thofe which were ſtruck in the time of the Roman
greatnefs. So that after Medals came to be regarded and ſtudied by the Moderns, few perfons
troubled themfelves with collecting thofe of the
Lower Empire; until by being neglected, fome
of them are become fcarce, and on that account,
valuable; as fome Books are, many copies of
which have been confumed by the *Cheeſe-mongers*
and *Paſtry-cooks*. The whole number of different
Imperial Medals, ſtill extant, is reckoned by *F.
Joubert* to be about one thoufand, or one thoufand two hundred of Gold; about three thoufand
of Silver; and fix or feven thoufand of Copper
and Brafs.

F   SECTION

SECTION the FOURTH:

OF THE

Impreſſion *and* Form

Of M E D A L S.

TO the Form belong the Inſcriptions and Figures, which are impreſſed upon Medals, ordinarily on both Sides or Tables.

The two Tables are diſtinguiſhed into the *Face* and *Reverſe;* each of which uſually bears a Fi-gure, and Inſcription: Uſually, I ſay; for ſome-times you have a Figure without any Inſcription; and ſometimes an Inſcription without any Figure.

The Circular Inſcription, near the edge of a Medal, is called the *Legend.* That on the Face commonly contains the Names, Titles, Offices, &c. of the Perſon whoſe head it bears: That on the Reverſe, either ſome Motto, refering to the virtues of the perſon to whoſe honour it was ſtruck, to ſome great action which he has per-formed,

formed, or to the benefits which the publick had reaped by him; or else, the Legend is the name of some Virtue, or Deity, reprefented by the Figure; or of fome Province, or Country, reprefented by fome Symbol or Emblem. Yet this diftinction betwixt the two Legends does not hold univerfally; for fometimes we find the Titles occupying both Tables, and fometimes the Motto. I have faid the Legend is the Circular Infcription near the edge of the Medal; but this is to be underflood only in the general: fome Legends being placed in a right line, either above, or below the Figure; or part above, and part below; or upon the Figure itfelf; and in feveral other forms, according to the fancy of the Workman. The Latin Legends are all read from the left to the right: But the Legends of fome Greek Medals are wrote the contrary way, from the right to the left. The letters on the Circular Legends are commonly placed with the bottoms inward; but fometimes, with the bottoms toward the edge.

Befides the two Legends, there is on many Medals, a fhort Infcription under the Figure on the Reverfe, called the *Exergum* or *Exergue*, as being εξ εργυ, out of the work, from which it is frequently feparated by a line over it. This Exergue

F 2　　　　　　　contains

contains fometimes the date of the Coin, exprefs-
ing in what Confulfhip of the Emperor it was
ftruck; as C O S. III. upon the reverfe of *Antoninus*. Sometimes it fignifies the place where it
was ftruck, and to which the Coin properly belonged, as S. M. AL. for *Signata moneta Alexan-
driæ*, upon the reverfe of *Licinius:* Sometimes the
name of a province, the reduction of which the
Medal is defigned to celebrate; as *Judea*, in the
reverfe of *Vefpatian.* Sometimes S. C. is put in
the Exergue, and fometimes other letters, which
the Modern Medalifts are not able to explain.
Befides the Legends and Exergue, you often meet
with other letters on the Table, or Field; as the
S. C. on Roman Medals; L. on Greek Medals,
with fome other letter or letters expreffing the
date. The Roman L being the antient Greek
Λ, is here faid to ftand for λυχιβαντ●-, a poe-
tical word for *Anno*.

Let us now attend to the Figures we fee on
Ancient Coins.

1ft. On the Face, where we commonly have
the Pourtrait of fome great and illuftrious Perfon; ufually, if not always, in profile. The Confular Medals have commonly the Heads of fome
of their Gods, or of their Ancient Kings, or of
Rome, which is a manly Face wearing a Helmet,

to

to exprefs her warlike genius; and winged, to denote her fpeedy and extenfive conquefts. The Heads of the Roman Kings are for the moft part dreffed with a Diadem; which was nothing more than a fillet bound round the head, the ends of which, being tied in a knot behind, fell down upon the neck. This was the proper badge and ornament of Kings, and was never worn by any of the Emperors till after *Conftantine*, when it was enriched with Pearls and Diamonds.

Julius Cæfar was the firft among the Romans who ftruck his own Head upon the Coin, in which he was followed by all the fucceeding Emperors. The proper drefs of the Imperial Head is a Crown, for the moft part of Laurel; the right of wearing which was decreed to *Julius Cæfar* by the Senate, and afterwards continued to his Succeffors. Befides thefe, feveral other Crowns of different fafhions, are found on Medals; fuch as the *Roftral Crown*, compofed of the Prows of Ships, which was given upon a naval victory. The *Mural Crown*, compofed of Towers; the reward of fuch as had taken Cities, and alfo the ornament of their Tutelar Deities. Crowns of Rays were beftowed on Princes when they were deified, either before, or after their death; as being properly the ornament of the Gods: Some

have

have fuppofed the Gentiles took the hint of thefe Radiated Crowns from fome tradition of the fhining of *Mofes*'s Face, which is mentioned, *Exod.* liv. 29. and this Phænomenon they conceived of as occafioned by Beams or Rays of light darting from his head. Indeed this feems to have been likewife the notion of the Vulgate Tranflator, who renders the word קָרַן *Cornuta;* not furely imagining that *Mofes* was really Horned, but that he appeared with rays of light, like Horns, emitted from his head.

The Emperor *Juftinian* was the firft who ufed an arched Crown, furmounted with a Crofs; fuch as is wore by Chriftian Kings at this day. Some Heads of Emperors are wholly naked; there are fuch of *Auguftus, Nero, Galba,* and fome others. Though more commonly a naked head, ftruck in the Imperial Ages, is a fign that it is not the Head of an Emperor, but of one of his Sons, or the Prefumptive Heir of the Empire.

The Heads of the Gods are diftinguifhed by their proper Crowns; as a Crown of Ears of Corn is a Symbol of *Ceres;* a Crown of Flowers denotes *Flora;* a Crown of Vine-Leaves or Ivy is the drefs of *Bacchus;* the *Petafus,* or Hat with two wings, belongs to *Mercury;* the Hat without brims is the mark of *Vulcan,* &c.

Heads

Heads are not only diftinguifhed by their drefs, but fometimes by certain Symbols attending them; as when we fee the *Lituus*, or Augural-Staff placed by the Head; which is the Symbol of the *Pontifex Maximus*. But fuch Symbols are more commonly found on the Reverfes, which we fhall treat of hereafter.

The Ancient Coins prefent us not only with the Pourtraits of Kings, and Emperors, and other great men, but alfo of Queens and other Ladies of high rank: chiefly the Wives of the Emperors. This honour, of having their Heads ftamped on the Coin, was done them either in their life time. or after their death; as on occafion of their Apotheofis or Confecration, fignified, by Peacocks on the reverfe. The Face of fome Medals is charged with two Heads, which are either fet Face to Face, as on the Medals of *Severus* and the Emprefs *Domna;* or Back to Back as on the Medal of *Julius Cæfar* and *Octavianus,* (after-wards called *Auguftus)* his adopted Son and Suc-ceffor; ftruck by the *Colonia Nemaufenfis,* in hon-our of *Auguftus,* upon his defeating *M. Antony* and *Cleopatra;* whereby he fubdued all *Egypt* to the Roman power, fignified by the device of a Crocodile chained to a Palm-tree. Some are ftamped with three Heads or more on the Face; but thefe are very uncommon.   We

We have obferved before that the *Titles* are generally upon the Face of the Medal, and we now proceed to confider them more particularly.

The titular addition to the proper name of the perfon whofe Head the Medal bears, ufually confifts, partly, of mere Titles of honour; fuch as *Imperator, Cæfar, Auguftus,* given to all the Roman Emperors after *Octavianus.* The Title of *Auguftus* was firft decreed to him by the Roman Senate, and was affumed by all his Succeffors, as *Augufta* was by their wives. *Cæfar* was originally the cognomen of the firft Roman Emperor *C. Julius Cæfar;* which by a decree of the Senate all fucceeding Emperors were to bear. But when the Title *Auguftus* was confered upon his immediate fucceffor, the Title *Cæfar* was given to the fecond perfon of the Empire, as to the prefumptive Heir of the Crown; notwithftanding it ftill continued to be applied to the Emperor himfelf. Hence we fee the difference betwixt *Cæfar* ufed fimply, and *Cæfar* with the addition of *Imperator Auguftus.*

Imperator was originally an appellation, with which the Soldiers complimented a victorious General; but it afterwards came to denote the Supreme Commander, or Head of the Empire. However, when we find a Number added to Imperator;

perator; as I M P. III. or IIII, it fignifies that he had acted as General in the Army, and had been faluted Imperator by the Soldiers, as many times as the number expreffes.

In the Lower Empire, the Title *Dominus* was firft affumed by *Aurelian*, and ufed by his Succeffors; on whofe Coins we often fee the Legend begin with D. N. for *Dominus Nofter:* Other Titles, affixed to proper names, are a fort of Sirnames, which the perfons virtues are fuppofed to have gained him; as *Pius,* a Title firft given to *Antoninus;* which *Commodus* alfo affumed; and added *Felix* to it: for which a thoufand abufes were paffed upon him. Again, *Pater Patriæ* was a Title firft beftowed on *Cicero,* for his difcovering and defeating the confpiracy of *Cataline;* and was afterwards affumed by the Emperors. *Pifcennius* took upon him the Sirname of *Juftus;* and *Dioclefian,* that of *Beatiffimus,* and *Feliciffimus; Trajan* had the Titles, *Optimus* and *Clemens,* decreed him by the Senate. *Conftantine* called himfelf *Maximus;* and *Victorinus* affected the Title of *Invictus.* Other Titles, again, are the names of Offices; as *Conful,* which in the time of the Emperors, was little, if any thing, more than a mere name; however the people were fond of keeping it up, accounting it fome remains or memento

G   of

of their Ancient Liberty ; and therefore the Emperors submitted to be chosen Consuls by the people. The number, which we often see added to C O S. signifies how many times the person had been thus elected; yet it is plain this Election was not always made annually, as in the time of the proper Consuls ; for the Emperor *Hadrian*'s Medals have for several years together C O S. III. upon them.

Another Title of Office is, *Tribunitia potestas;* which, in the time of the Roman Commonwealth, was the highest authority ; for the Tribunes of the people had power to annul the decrees of the Senate, and nothing could be concluded without their consent; nay, they have sometimes called the Consuls and Dictators to account for their conduct before the people. This power and title was first assumed by the Emperor *Augustus;* and afterwards, generally, by his Successors.

The year of the Tribuneship is commonly expressed after the Title, as T R I B. P O T. X. or XVI, &c. which yet does not always denote the year of the Emperor's reign; for sometimes, though rarely, this power was given to another besides the Emperor; as to the Presumptive Heir of the Empire. Hence it is that the year of the T R I B. P O T. expressed in the Title, is sometimes

times a much higher number than the year of the Emperor's reign. Thus *Vespatian* gave the *Tribunitia Potestas* to his Son *Titus,* two years after he was made Emperor. We therefore see on the Medals of *Titus,* TRIB. POT. X. or XV. though he reigned but three years after his Father. Other examples of the same kind occur in *Marcus Aurelius, Caracalla, Geta,* &c. The Office of *Pontifex Maximus* was also constantly assumed by the Roman Emperors, and generally expressed among their Titles, from *Augustus* down to *Constantine,* by whom it was refused. It was afterwards reassumed by *Julian,* but quite laid aside by *Gratian;* after whom no Emperor has P. M. in his Titles. *Julius Cæsar* assumed the Title of *Dictator Perpetuus. Claudius* took upon him the Office of *Censor,* and *Domitian* made himself *Censor Perpetuus;* as appears upon their Coins.

It is to be observed, that these Names and Titles are expressed in different Cases; sometimes in the Nomnative Case, as *Cæsar Augustus;* sometimes in the Genitive, as *Divi Julii;* which Case is chiefly used in the Greek Medals, as βασιλεως Αλεξανδρυ ; as if εικων, or νομισμα was understood; that is the Image or Coin of *Alexander.* Sometimes the Name is put in the Dative Case; as IMP. *Nervæ, Trojano, Germanico,* &c. It is

rarely

rarely put in the Accufative, in the Latin; though there is an inſtance of that fort in a Medal of *Gallienus;* inſcribed *Gallienum Auguſtum;* but it is more common in the Greek.

The Titles are hardly ever wrote at length, but contraſtedly, by one or more of the initial letters of each word; as A U G. for *Auguſtus;* C Æ S. for *Cæſar;* C Æ S S. for *Cæſares;* C O S S. for *Conſules;* P P. for *Pater Patriæ;* P.F. for *Pius Felix,* &c. Mr. *Patin,* in his *Hiſtoria Numiſmatum,* hath given us a Table of Roman abreviations uſed on Medals; which Mr. *Evelin,* in his *Numiſmata,* hath ſomewhat enlarged. You have alſo a Table of a great number of theſe abreviations at the end of *Ainſworth*'s and *Littleton*'s Dictionaries.

Secondly. We proceed to take a view of the Reverſe of Medals, in which the chief Erudition of this Science lies.

Of theſe there is ſuch a vaſt variety, eſpecially of the Imperial Medals, that one is at a loſs which to ſingle out for a ſpecimen of the whole. As for the Conſular Medals, which we ſhall treat of in the firſt place; the ſame Reverſe is common to many of them; as *Caſtor* and *Pollux* on horſe back, which is ſaid to be the Reverſe that was firſt in uſe; then of Victory, or one of the Gods; or the Perſon to whoſe honour the Medal was ſtruck,

ſtruck, driving a chariot with two or four horſes; whence the Denarii with theſe Reverſes, were diſtinguiſhed into Bigati and Quadrigati. The *Ratis* alſo, or Ship; or perhaps the Prow of the Ship, as the Emblem of Naval Power, was no uncommon Reverſe on the Conſular Coins; whence the pieces with this impreſſion were called *Ratiti.* Beſides theſe, ſuch Conſular Medals as bore on the Face the Imprefs of their Ancient Kings, often preſerved on the Reverſe the memory of ſome worthy action they had performed; as that of K. *Ancus* has, on the Reverſe, the famous Aqueduct, with the Equeſtrian Statue upon it, by which the *Aqua Martia* was brought nine miles to *Rome*, and which was begun by this *Ancus.* Medals ſtruck on the occaſion of founding Colonies, have ſometimes, on the Reverſe, a prieſt following a Yoke of Oxen, and perhaps with a Plough; ſignifying the manner in which the boundaries of the Colonies was marked out; or ſome ſay the Oxen are deſigned to intimate, that the Colony was planted by the common people; whereas the Trophies we ſometimes ſee on the Reverſes of theſe Medals, ſignify they were planted by the Veteran Soldiers.

2*dly.* The Reverſes of Imperial Medals are ſo different and various, according to the humours

or

or fancies of the Princes or Mint-Maſters by whoſe direction they were ſtruck; that one knows not how to range them into any claſs or order. However the chief of them may be reduced to three heads, viz. *Figures*, or *Perſonages; Publick Monuments*; or *Buildings;* and *Inſcriptions.*

1ſt. The Figures or Perſonage, which we ſo commonly ſee on the Reverſes of Medals, are ſometimes of Princes; ſometimes the ſame in Miniature, whoſe pourtrait is more at large on the Face: as on the Reverſes of the Emperors of the Family of *Conſtantine*, one often ſees the Emperor ſtanding with a *Labarum* in his right hand, and a Globe, ſurmounted with a Victory, in his left. The *Labarum* was the Imperial ſtandard, embroidered and ſet with precious Stones; which in the time of the Chriſtian Emperors, inſtead of an Eagle formerly embroidered upon it, had the Monogram of Jeſus Chriſt; viz. the two firſt letters of the word χρις⊙ expreſſed in a cypher thus ☧ Sometimes the Emperor appears in the Reverſe, diſguiſed under the Figure of ſome God; as on the Reverſe of a *Dioclefian*, who had aſſumed the name of *Jovius*, he appears in the Figure of *Jupiter*, ſitting in a chair, with a Globe in his hand, ſurmounted with a Victory: the Legend *Jovi.* H. U. C C. i. e. *Hoc voluerunt conſules.*

Sometimes

Sometimes the Figure on the Reverfe, is fome relation of that on the Face, as *Auguflus* on the Reverfe of *Julius;* and *Claudius* on the Reverfe of his mother *Antonia.* We fometimes fee on the Reverfe the Figure of fome God, either of him to whofe worfhip the Emperor was more efpecially devoted; or of him whofe protection and bleffing was in a peculiar manner fupplicated for him; as *Minerva* on the Reverfe of a *Domitian ;* and on the Reverfe of *Mar. Aurelius,* the Goddefs *Salus,* with a *Patera* in her hand, facrificing to *Æfculapius,* who was worfhiped in the form of a ferpent. Again, the virtues for which the Emperor was, or defired to be celebrated, are not uncommonly expreffed by the Figures on Reverfes; as *Virtue,* or *Courage,* on the Reverfe of a *Domitian,* reprefented by a bold armed Woman with a fpear in her right hand, and a *Parazonium* in her left; the Legend *Virtuti Augufli. Liberty,* on the Reverfe of a *Commodus,* carrying in her right hand the Cap of Liberty; and in her left, the Wand called *Rudis,* or *Vindicta;* which was laid on the head of a flave when he was made free: *Equity,* on the Reverfe of a *Vefpatian,* with a fpear in her right hand, and a balance in her left.

The virtues of the Ladies are alfo celebrated on the Reverfes of their Medals; as piety on the
Reverfe

Reverfe of a *Fauflina*, in the Habit of a veftal virgin, ftrewing Frankincenfe on an altar; *Fecunditas* on the Reverfe of an other Medal of the fame Lady: *Spes Reipublicæ* on the Reverfe of *Maximiana Faufla*, fecond wife of *Conflantine* the great; expreffed by a Female Figure, with a Helmet on to reprefent the Republic, and two children at her breafts. Mr. *Addifon* has given us a collection of thefe forts of Figures in his *firfl Series.*

Provinces are alfo reperfented by Figures and Perfonages; to fignify either the Emperor's conquefts, or his care of them: as *Judea*, on the Reverfe of a *Vefpatian*, fitting in a melancholy pofture at the bottom of a pillar adorned with Trophies, to fignify her captive ftate. *Dacia*, on the Reverfe of *Hadrianus*, fitting on a Rock, holding an Eagle in her right hand, and a Branch in her left. *Italia*, on the Reverfe of *Commodus*, with a *Cornu Copia* in her right hand, to denote her fruitfulnefs; a *Crown of Towers* on her head, to figure out the many Cities that ftand upon her; a Scepter in her left hand, and fitting on a Globe, to fhew fhe is Sovereign of Nations. See a Collection of thefe fort of Figures in Mr. *Addifon's third Series.*

Sometimes the Figure is intended to immortalize

talize fome worthy action of the Emperor. As his enriching the Nation, or his care about the Publick Coin, is fignified, on the Reverfe of a *Domitian*, by the Goddefs *Moneta*, with a *Cornu Copia* in her left hand, and a *Balance* in her right. On Reverfes we have not only a variety of fingle Figures; but fometimes two, three, or more; as *Honos* and *Virtus* on the Reverfe of *Galba*, in Mr. *Addifon's Firft Series, Medal the fecond.* And on a Medal of *Trajan's* are feen three Kings, and the Emperor crowning them. On one of *Hadrian's* there are eight Figures, but without any Legend to explain them; and on one of *Commodus* there are ten.

Before we difmifs this head concerning the Figures on Medals, it will be proper to take notice of other animals, often met with on Reverfes, which have alfo their fignification; as the *Eagle* and the *Peacock* denote the confecration of Princes and Princeffes, when they were admitted into the number of the Gods; the *Crocodile* is the Symbol of *Egypt*; a *Serpent* of *Æfculapius*; *Arabia* is marked by a *Camel*; *Spain* by a *Rabbit*, (a creature which abounds in that country;) *Mauritania* is known by a *Horfe* and *Switch*, fignifying the fwiftnefs of its Courfers; *Elephants* in trapings are to be feen on the Reverfe of an *Antoninus Pius*, and a *Severus*; which imports, that thefe Emperors procured

H   thofe

thofe creatures to entertain the people at the publick fhews. We have alfo fabulous Animals and
Monfters; as the *Griffion* on the Reverfe of a Medal of *Gallienus*; a *Centaur* on another of the
fame Emperor; and a *Phænix* on fome Medals of
Conftantine and his Sons; to denote, what it feems
they hoped for and expected, the perpetuity of
the Empire.

2*d.* The fecond fort of Reverfes are publick
Monuments and Buildings; as the Temple of
Janus fhut, on the Reverfe of a *Nero*; to fignify
the univerfal peace he gave to the Empire; The
Macellum, (or a view of the Shambles which he
caufed to be built for the convenience of the public) on another of the fame Emperor; The fump-
tuous Bridge which *Trajan* built over the *Tiber*,
adorns the Reverfe of one of his Medals; The
Amphitheatre of *Titus*, and his *Naval Column*, are
to be feen on his. The *Port*, or *Gate of a City*,
which is found on the Reverfe of fome Medals,
with the Legend *PROVIDENTIA AUGUSTI*, or
CÆSARIS, is a Monument of the Emperor's muni-
ficence and care in providing a Magazine of Corn
for the People in a time of fcarcity. If a *Star* appears over the gate, it denotes *Conftantinople*. Such
a Reverfe we have on the Emperor *Conftantinus*,
junior, the Legend *PROVIDENTIÆ CÆSS.*

3*d.* The third fort of Reverfes are infcriptions
on

on the Table or Field of the Medal. Of this fort
there are feveral Latin and Greek Imperial Medals, which have nothing on the Reverfe but
S. C. or Δ. E. for δημαρχικης εξυσιας, inclofed
in a Crown. Others fet forth great Occurrences, as
VICTORIA GERMANICA, IMP. VI. COS. III.
on the Reverfe of *M. Aurelius.* Others have Titles
of Honour granted to the Princes; as S. P. Q. R,
OPTIMO PRINCIPI, on the Reverfe of a *Trajan;*
and alfo of an *Antoninus Pius.* Other infcriptions
have refpect to public vows, which were made for
the Emperor every ten years; or (fometimes in the
lower Empire) every five years; which, according to Mr. *Du Cange* had their rife from *Auguftus's*
pretending to be defirous of quitting the Empire:
but at the requeft of the Senate, he twice con-
fented to continue the Government for ten years
longer; upon which it became a cuftom at every
ten years, to make publick Prayers, Sacrifices,
and Games,. for the prefervation of the Emperor.
Hence we fee the Reverfe of a *Conftantius, VOTIS*
XXX; *MULTIS* XXXX. importing (as I apprehend) not only that he might reign thirty years,
or ten years more, from the time when the vows
were made, namely, when he had already reigned
twenty years, but that they engaged to make new
vows at the expiration of thirty years, that he
might reign forty years; for it cannot mean that
he

he had reigned thirty years at the time when the vows were made, since he died in the twenty-sixth year of his reign. This custom lasted until *Theodo-sius;* after whom no such Epocha is to be found.

Besides the Reverses which we have ranged into these three Classes, there are many others which cannot be reduced to any of them; such as *Addison* calls *Riddles.* For instance, on the Reverse of an *Augustus,* Mercury in the form of a *Terminus,* standing on a Thunderbolt; which was probably intended for a *Rebus,* to express the sense of that Emperor's Motto, *Festina lente.* The *Terminus* was a Figure without either Arms, Hands, or Feet; signifying, says *Polybius,* that all quarrels and contests about the limits and boundaries, were determined. Instruments of Religion were Symbols of the *Pontifex Maximus,* and signified the Piety of the Prince, on whose Coin they were born. Thus upon a Reverse of *Nerva,* we see the *Lituus,* the *Simpulum,* the *Asperforium,* and the *Capula.* Two hands joining one another, holding two Ears of Corn, and a *Caduceus* betwixt them, on the Reverse of a *Titus,* import the good harmony and union betwixt the Prince and the Publick; the Peace arising from such an union, and the Plenty which is the Fruit of such a Peace. See a collection of this sort of Reverses in *Addison*'s *second Series.*

SECTION

SECTION the FIFTH:

OF THE

VALUE and USE

Of MEDALS.

Firft. THE value of Medals, in common computation, is rated not by the Metal, or Size, nor merely by their Antiquity, but by their Rarity. The Metal is of fo little confideration, that a Copper Medal is fometimes valued at a much higher rate than a Silver, or a Gold one: For inftance, the Copper *Otho,* of the larger fize, called a *Singular Medal,* becaufe there is fuppofed to be but *one,* or however very few of them in the world; is of almoft ineftimable value; while a Gold one fhall not fell for above two or three Guineas more than its weight. And if a piece of King *Numa's* Leather Money could now be found, it would, no doubt, be valued above any Gold one. Such a fingular Coin is a

Silver

Silver Greek Medailion of *Pefcennius*, which is in the *French* King's Cabinet. Hence the Medals of thofe Emperors, who reigned a fhorter time, are generally more valued than thofe that reigned longer; becaufe there were fewer of them ftruck, and they are therefore the rarer. Yet fometimes an uncommon. Reverfe fhall give a great value to a Medal, whofe Head, with another Reverfe, is very common.

In colle&ing of Medals great caution is to be ufed, that we are not impofed upon by counterfeits; efpecially of fuch Medals as are fcarce and rare. For that purpofe we muft attend to the Field, and obferve whether it is fmooth, and free from marks of the fand which may commonly be feen on caft Medals: to the letters and Figures which are never fo fharp and clean in caft Medals as in ftamped ones; to the Edges, to obferve whether there be any marks of the file, which has been ufed in a caft Medal; efpecially in that part where the Metal ran into the mould. We are to obferve again, whether there be any cracks in the Edges; for though the abfence of them be no certain fign of a counterfeit; yet, when they are found, they are looked upon as pretty good indications' of the Medals being genuine. But nothing is more to be regarded than
the

the *Colour* and *Varnifh*, efpecially of Copper Medals; many of which have a certain inimitable
Varnifh and Politure; fome *Green*, fome *Blue*,
others of a *Redifh Brown;* which whether it was
given them by art, or has been contracted by age,
is not abfolutely determined: though the latter
feems more probable, fince all the art of the
falfifiers, whether by *Sal Armoniack, Vinegar,*
burning Paper upon them, burying them in the
Earth, or any other way, has by no means
equaled it. There is indeed a Green Varnifh,
which is commonly ufed for this purpofe, that
is pretty enough; but it is too bright and glaring;
fo that a little experience will enable a perfon to
diftinguifh it from the antique.

Secondly. As to the Ufe of Ancient Medals, befides a thoufand little impertinences, as *Addifon*
calls them, that are very gratifying to curiofity,
fuch as the drefs of the moft celebrated Ladies of
antiquity, the flattering titles affected by this and
the other Emperor, and the honours he payed
to his family and friends; the adepts in *Phyfiog-*
nomy would not forgive me, if I fhould not alfo
mention in this clafs, the Features and Linia-
ments of fo many illuftrious perfonages as are
to be met with in Statues and Medals. But befides thefe and many other like matters of mere,

yet

yet very entertaining curiofity, they are capable of feveral more fubftantial ufes; concerning which the learned *Spanheim* has publifhed a large Volume, *De Prestantia et ufu Numifmatum Antiquarum:* For inftance, they are of very confiderable fervice in Hiftory; for befides, that many facts and events, not recorded by any of the ancient Hiftorians, may be collected from them, they throw great light on feveral obfcure paffages in thofe writers. And indeed there is hardly any confiderable event in the Græcian or Roman Hiftory, to which fome reference may not be found in the Coins of thofe Nations. So that a Cabinet of Medals may be confidered as in a manner a Body of Hiftory; being converfant with which will fix hiftorical facts and circumftances upon the memory with more eafe, as well as give a greater degree of certainty concerning them, than Books alone will ordinarily do.

Chronology receives not a little aid from Medals, as they not only perpetuate the memory of Illuftrious Actions, but often mark the Year when they were performed.

Geography hath been greatly beholden to this Science, for afcertaining the Names of Ancient Places, the Founders of Cities and Colonies; and fometimes their fituation, by the neighbour-
hood

hood of fome noted river, mountain, &c. expreſſed
by fome device on a Medal.

By the help of Medals we difcover what honours and privileges certain Cities were anciently
poſſeſſed of.   For inſtance, we learn from them,
what Cities, befides *Rome*, had the Privilege of
Roman Citizens. The honour of a City's being
νεωχορ℗ is celebrated on many Grecian Medals; which imports that it had a temple in it,
where the folemn facrifices of the whole province
were performed for their Prince, and public
games were exhibited to his honour, as often as
his permiſſion could be obtained for that purpofe.
Hence we fee on fome Medals ΔIC, TPIC,
TETPAKIC, &c. ΝΕΩΚΟΡΩΝ. For though
the word νεωχορ℗, derived from ναℇ, *templum*,
and χωρεω, *verro*, *purgo*, doubtlefs imported originally a mean office, namely, that of a *Sacriſtan*,
or *Sexton;* yet in time it came to be a term or
title of honour, importing not only the celebra-
tion of the Games (as we have faid before,) but
alfo the religious devotion of a city to fome
Deity: in which fenfe it is applied to the City
of *Epheſus*, Acts xix. 35. faid to be νεωκορον της
μεγαλης Θεας Αρτεμιδℇ, και του Διοπετυς:
and therefore I apprehend, more properly rendered
in that place *cultricem* in the Vulgate, and *Wor-*
I   *ſhiper*

fhiper in our Engliſh tranſlation, than *Ædituam;* as in *Beza,* and in ſome others.

We learn alſo from Medals, in many caſes, which was the chief City or Metropolis of a Province; and in what ſenſe a City is called ϖρωτη, when it was not the Metropolis, as *Phi-lippi* is ſaid to be, πρωῐη της μεριδ῀῀ της Μακε-δονιας πολις, κολωνια, Acts xvi. 12. That *Phi-lippi* was a Roman Colony, appears from a Medal ſtruck in the reign of *Claudius,* with this Legend, COL. AUG. IVL. PHILIP. that is, *Colonia Auguſta Julia Philippi,* or *Philippenſis.* And in what ſenſe this City was πρωτη πολις, though *Theſſalonica* was undoubtedly the Metropolis or chief City of the Province, may be gathered from the uſe of the word πρωτη, as applied to ſeveral other Cities on Ancient Coins: as in the pro-conſular *Aſia,* not only *Epheſus,* which was the chief City, but *Smyrna,* and *Pergamus,* have the title πρωτη: and in *Bythinia,* not only *Nicomedia,* which was the Metropolis; but *Nicea* is alſo called πρωτη. Now, *Spanheim* ſhews; that this title, when thus applied to inferior Cities, refers to the Games which ſeveral Cities joined in ſupporting, and of which one was the πρωτη. In this ſenſe *Philippi* was the πρωτη πολις, (not της επαρχιας, but της μεριδ῀῀,) of a particular diſtrict of *Macedonia.* I

I have not yet mentioned all the Arts and Sciences which receive light and aid from Medals. Sculpture and Painting have revived, in later ages, along with this Study; to which those Arts are greatly indebted for noble hints and patterns. The same may be said of Architecture, which now borrows its finest ornaments from the Plans and Models of Ancient Temples, Ports, Triumphal Arches, and other public Edifices, preserved on Medals. Mr. *Addison* has abundantly convinced us of their use to explain numerous passages in the Classics. By their means the Natural Philosopher also acquaints himself with a great variety of foreign Plants and Animals. And the Divine, not only finds the usefulness of Medals, for explaining and illustrating several Texts of Scripture, as we have seen above; but hereby he informs himself of the Ancient Theology of the Greeks and Romans: Here he sees the Gods they worshiped, and their Attributes expressed in significative Emblems; here he sees their Altars and Adorations; and the Instruments with which they performed their sacred Rites. Upon the whole, therefore, though it cannot be denied that some persons have carried the Study of Medals to a ridiculous extravagance; yet it by no means deserves to be treated with the contempt it is by others, or to be wholly neglected.

F I N I S.

Preparing for the Press,

A Syſtem of JEWISH ANTIQUITIES;
IN
A Courſe of LECTURES on the three Firſt
Books of *Godwin's Moſes* and *Aaron.*

To which is annexed,

A DISSERTATION on the
HEBREW LANGUAGE.

BY

The late Rev. *DAVID JENNINGS,* D. D.

E R R A T A.

Page 7, *line* 14, *for* Epron. *read* Ephron *p.* 9,
l. 14, *after* than, *inſert* the Times of the *p.* 9, *l.* 23,
for Aben, Ezra, *r.* Aben-Ezra *p.* 11, *l.* 10, *for*
αργυριον, *r.* αργυριου *p.* 11, *l.* 17, *for* a certain,
r. of a certain *p.* 13. *l.* 15, *for* Opobulſumum.
r. Opobalſamum *p.* 14, *l.* 15, *for* דרבכנים, *r.*
דרכמנים *p.* 16. *l.* 24. *for* eighty four. Five, *r.*
eighty four, five *p.* 17. *l.* 14, 15, *for* Aurius, *r.*
Aureus *p.* 17, *l.* 16, 17, *for* Semiſſes and Tremiſ-
ſes, *r.* Semiſſis and Tremiſſis *p.* 18. *l.* 1, *for* ther,
r. their *p.* 18, *l.* 18, *for* C.O.N *r.* CON. *p.* 19,
l. 1, *after* with the, *inſert* Letters *p.* 20, *l.* 6. *after*
Braſs, *put a* Colon *p.* 22. *l* 26, *for* defines, *r.* defines *p.* 31, *l.* 26. *for* Conſul, *r.* Conſuls *p.* 32,
l. 9, *after* yet, *inſert* to *p.* 43, *laſt l. for* Trojano, *r.* Trajano *p.* 51, *l.* 21, *after* ſee, *inſert* on
p. 56, *l.* 4, 5, *for* Antiquarum, *r.* Antiquorum.